ANIMAL MAZES

Kim Blundell and Jenny Tyler

This book contains a series of mazes and maze-type puzzles. You can have fun doing these over and over again, as long as you don't write in the book. Trace the route with your finger, or, for the more difficult puzzles, put a piece of thin, see-through paper over the page and trace the route with a pencil.

Cat's rich cousin Lionel has invited Cat and Mouse to a party on his new island.

"He's sent two train tickets to Felixham, wherever that is," says Cat.

"And a complicated map," says Mouse. "I do wish Lionel would stop buying these cheap islands that are so difficult to find."

"Mmm. He does have good parties though," says Cat.

Cat looks at the map. "It's easy," he says. "The dotted lines are paths and the wiggly lines are ferry routes. We can rent a boat, too, and take it where we like. Come on."

He dashes off to sort out his party clothes and find a present for Lionel. Mouse is still looking at the map, frowning. "What's Lionel's island called?" he shouts.

"They're always named after him," shouts back Cat.

Can you help Cat and Mouse find their way to Lionel's island? Help them find the island and Felixham station first.

Dear Cat and Mouse

Please come to a summer party on my new island on Friday. Here's a map. Don't forget to mention my name when you see Nelson at Renta Boat.

From your cousin,
Lionel B. Cross

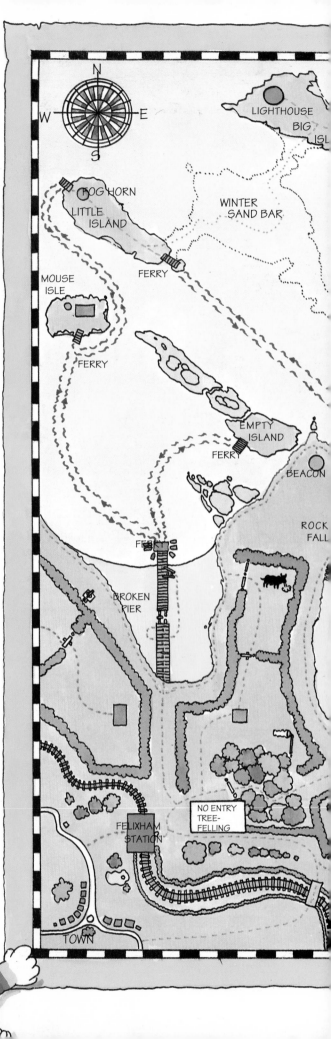

When Cat and Mouse arrive at Cross Isle, they find a note stuck to the pier.

"Party at lighthouse."

They set off along the hedge-lined paths, but soon realize that there are lots of animals hiding in corners, getting ready for the party.

They decide to choose their route very carefully so that they don't embarrass any of them by walking past the entrances to their hiding places.

Can you help them decide which way to go?

Welcome to Cross Isle

Party at lighthouse

4

Lionel is waiting for them at the lighthouse with his bodyguard, Vera Viper and a sad-looking penguin, called Pinkie. Pinkie seems worried that all the other animals are in pairs, and he is alone. (It is difficult to understand as he speaks Penguinese.)

Cat says, "Don't worry Pinkie. Wait here. We'll find a friend for you. Um, which way is it to Penguinland?"

"Try asking Surf Crab," says Lionel.

Before you follow Cat and Mouse, can you spot all the animal pairs?

Cat and Mouse follow the swampy smell and the signs for Surf Crab's hut. At last, they see it. Cat rushes on eagerly and falls straight into the swamp. Mouse helps him out.

They see they must pick their way carefully across the wobbly rocks and rickety bridges. They need you to help them find the way?

Unknown to Cat and Mouse (and to each other) both Pinkie and the sinister Vera Viper have decided to follow them.

See if you can spot them hiding in all the pictures from now on.

SURF CRAB'S HUT

SURF CRAB'S HUT

Surf Crab's hut is perched on the end of an old pier. Cat and Mouse can see Crab's fishing rod, but he doesn't seem to hear their shouts. They reluctantly decide that if they want an answer to their question, they will have to climb along the rotten and unsafe wood of the pier.

Can you help them find the way? They can walk across rocks and boats if they need to. (They cannot untie the boats though.)

Surf Crab doesn't know where Penguinland is either. He suggests Cat and Mouse ask Queen Conger and he lends them some diving equipment so they can go and see her.

She won't speak to them unless they take her some of the ripe red coral berries that grow on yellow and green striped seaweed. Blue and yellow berries give her a tummyache. Crab tells them to follow a piece of yellow and green striped seaweed that has only red berries growing on it. This should lead them to Queen Conger's cave. Can you help them?

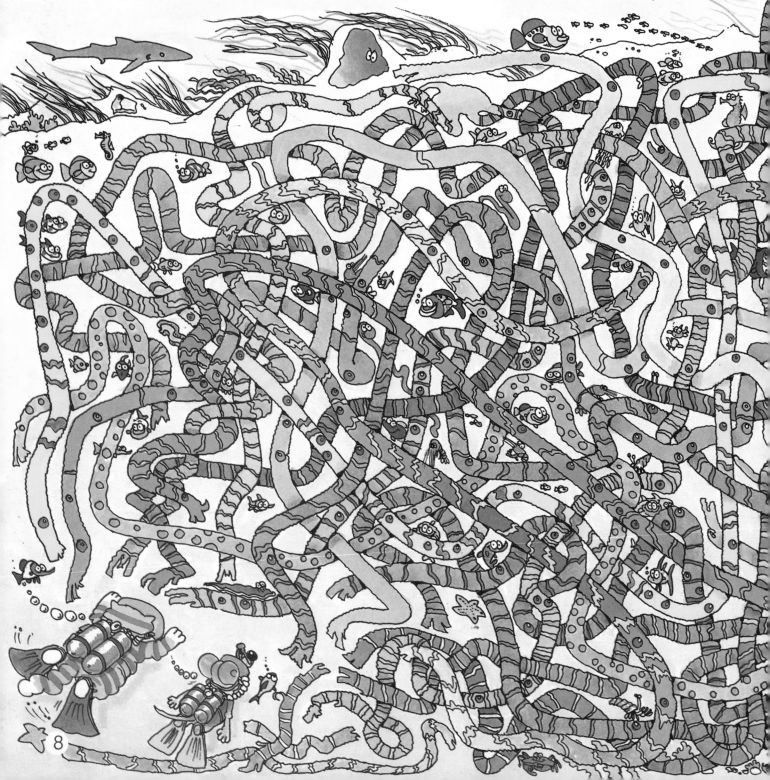

Queen Conger says she does know where Penguinland is, but she's not going to tell them because they didn't bring her enough berries. All she will say is that Cat and Mouse should swim to the wreck of the Angry Kipper and then go to the surface.

They must swim along underwater pathways to avoid the patrolling sharks that will bite their tails. Also, they must always swim past the seaweed not through it, because of the poisonous nose-nippers that live in it.

Help Cat and Mouse find their way to the Angry Kipper wreck.

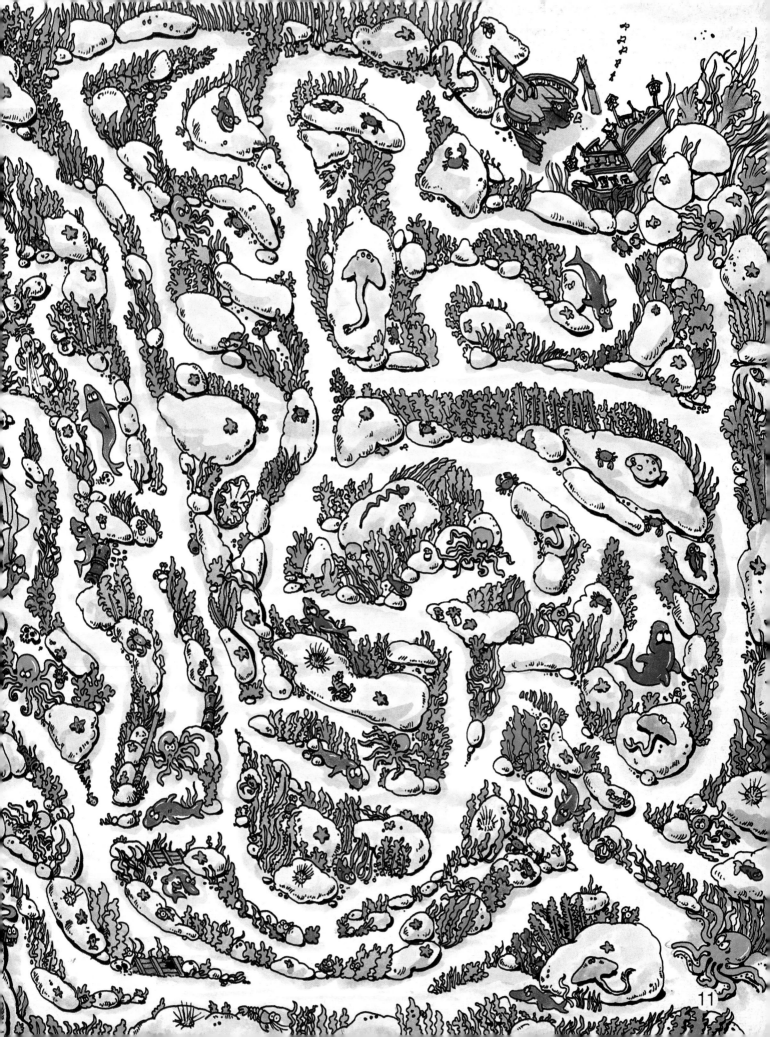

When Cat and Mouse rise to the surface, they see a toad sunbathing. They ask about Penguinland and he says, "My Grandpa will tell you. He's on the other side of the Lily Lagoon."

Mouse jumps into a lily flower and paddles it through the leaves to Grandpa Toad. Can you see which way he went?

Cat tries to do the same but he is too heavy and his flower sinks. He finds that the dark green lily leaves will stand his weight as long as they have no more than one hole in them. Help him find a pathway across the leaves. He can step over small gaps.

12

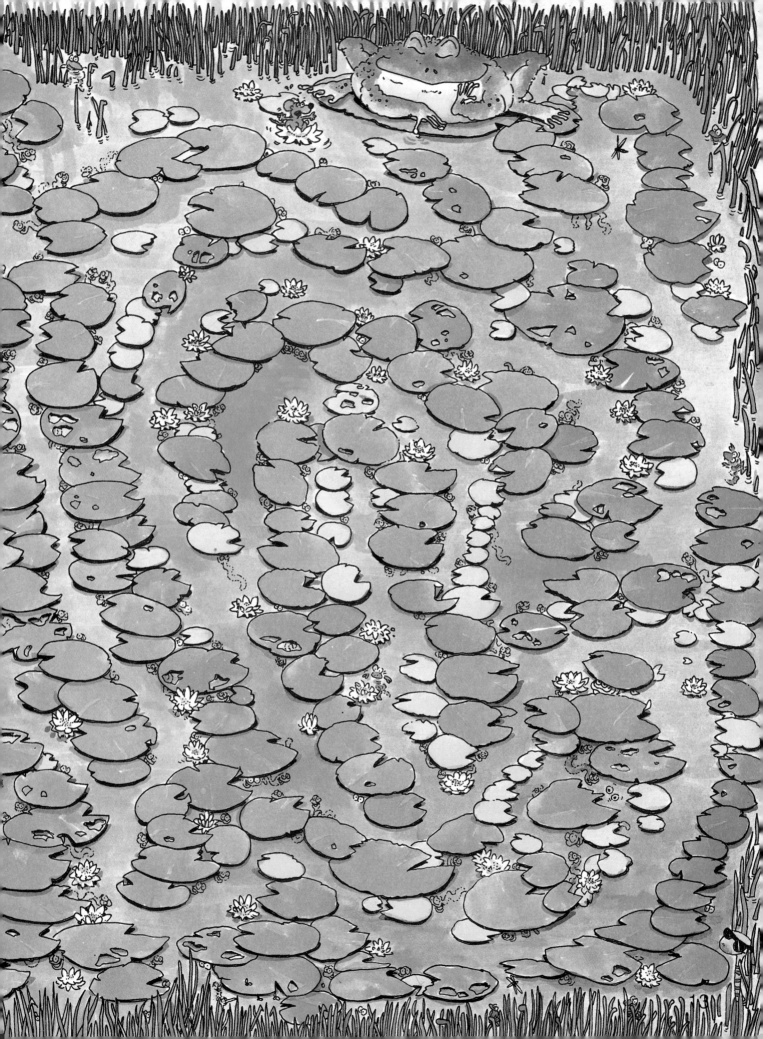

Cat and Mouse are surprised to find that Grandpa Toad is friendly. He tells them to speak to Pandora the Parrot and points to the tree where she lives.

There are lots of parrots in the tree. They ask which one is Pandora. It seems that her identical sisters have gone to Lionel's party and she is sulking near the top of the tree. Mouse must climb up carefully, crossing from one branch to another where they touch. The parrots will not move to let him pass by.

Which parrot is Pandora? Which way should Mouse climb to reach her?

Pandora is pleased to have something exciting to do.

"You must go up the mountain," she says. "I will lead you to the mountain steps."

She is too quick for Cat and Mouse, though. Can you help them find their way through the maze of rocks and bushes to the mountain steps?

Pandora is waiting for them, looking bored. "What took you two so long?" she yawns. "I'm going now. Talk to Eagle. He's over there on the Black Forest Plateau."

Mouse looks at the mountain in despair, but fears they would never find their way back to Lionel's and must go on.

"You must find a route which avoids the nests of flying lizards and dinosaurs. They get very angry if they are disturbed," screeches Pandora as she flies off.

Help Cat and Mouse find a safe route along the treacherous mountain paths.

Black Forest
Plateau

17

Gasping for breath in the thin air, Cat and Mouse find Eagle having his afternoon nap. They wake him and he tells them that the ice cap they can see in the distance is Penguinland.

"I've made a flume ride down the mountain," he says. "Choose a boat."

Cat looks puzzled. "I can't see any boats." Eagle points to some logs.

"Oh no," says Cat.

"We'll take number six," says Mouse.

"How clever of you to choose the deluxe twin-seater turbo model," says Eagle.

Help Cat and Mouse find their way down to the sea. They must always travel in the direction of the arrows, as these show the way the water flows.

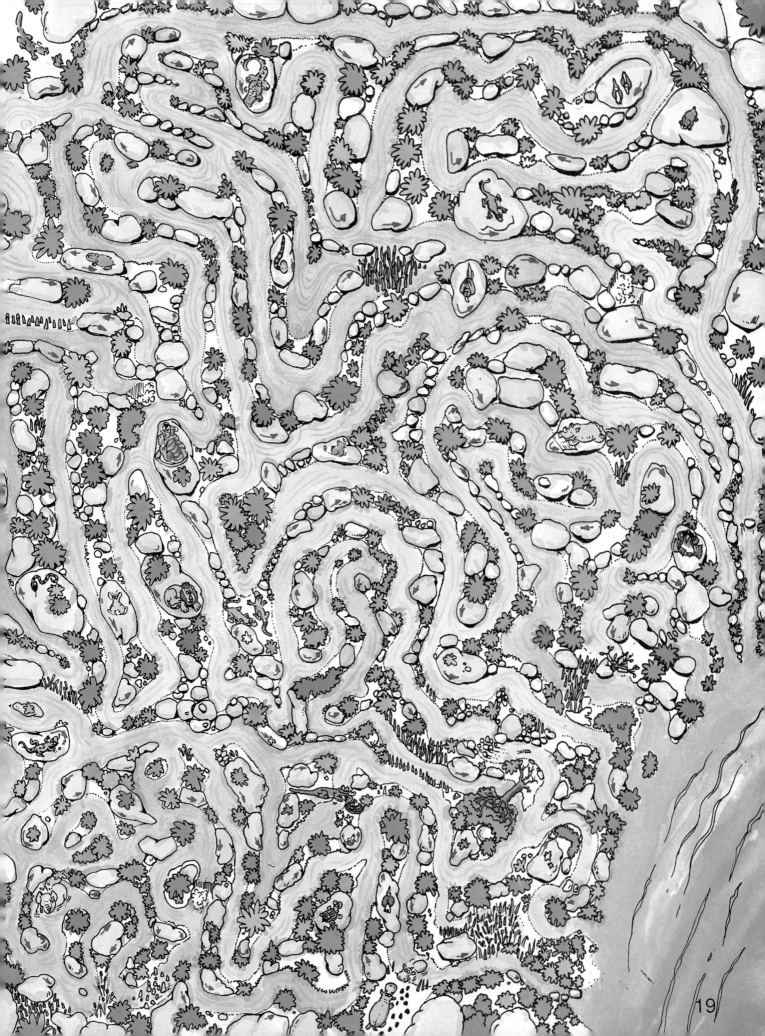

"Brrrr it's cold down here," says Cat. Let's find a quick way through all this ice. They find paddles attached to the side of the log.

"This must be the turbo part," says Mouse.

They paddle as fast as they can in the direction of Penguinland but find they must keeping twisting and turning to avoid the ice. Can you help them find the way through the ice to Penguinland?

"Penguinland at last!" exclaims Cat as they land. They hurriedly make for the group of pink penguins, following the tracks. After one painful attack they decide they must start again, dodging all the animals holding fish. The animals seem to want to hit them and the fish are deep-frozen so they hurt. Help Cat and Mouse find the way along the tracks to the penguins.

"Thank you for bringing Pinkie back to us," says King Penguin. Cat and Mouse look at each other in surprise as they realize that Pinkie has been following them.

"We must get back to Lionel's party," they gasp.

"Oh that won't take long," says King Penguin. "You didn't come the long way, I hope. We have a daily plane service to Felixham.

"Where's the plane," says Cat.

"Floating in the sea. What a pity you can't swim."

Can you help Cat and Mouse find a way to the sea plane? You may have to remind them how to get to Cross Isle from Felixham too.

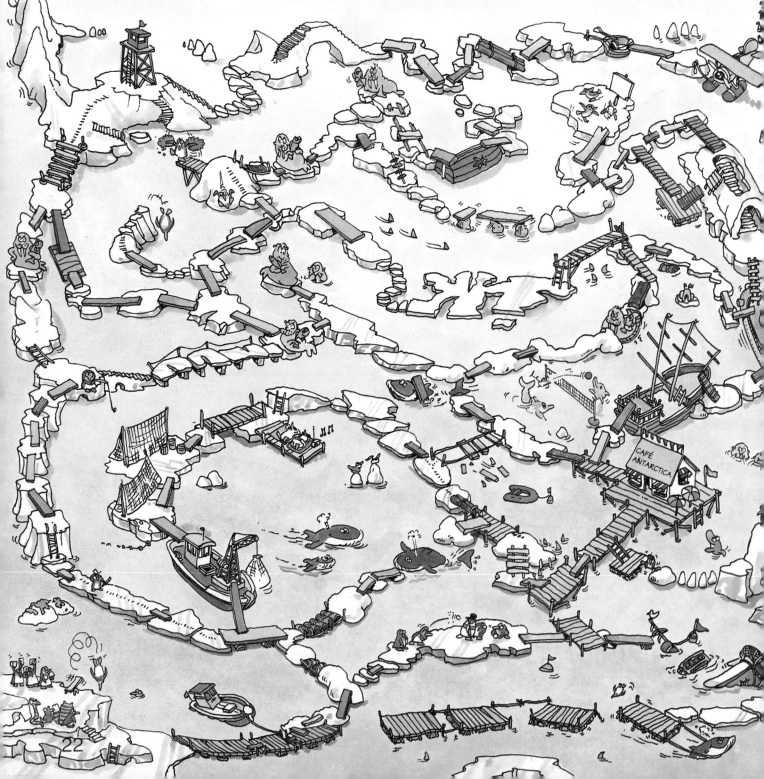

Answers

The red lines show the routes through the mazes.

Pages 2-3

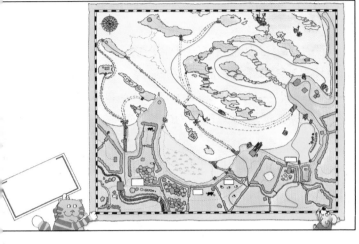

Pages 4-5

Page 6

Page 7

Pages 8-9

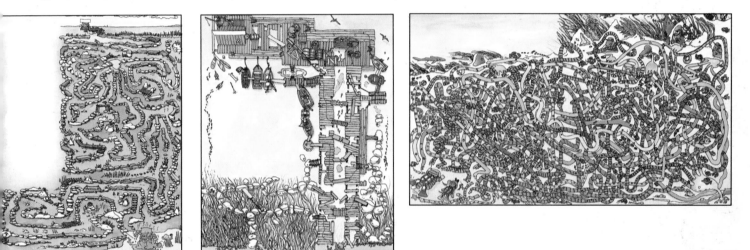

Pages 10-11

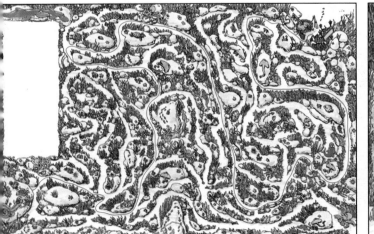

Pages 12-13

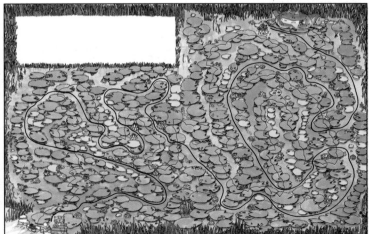

Page 14

Page 15

Pages 16-17

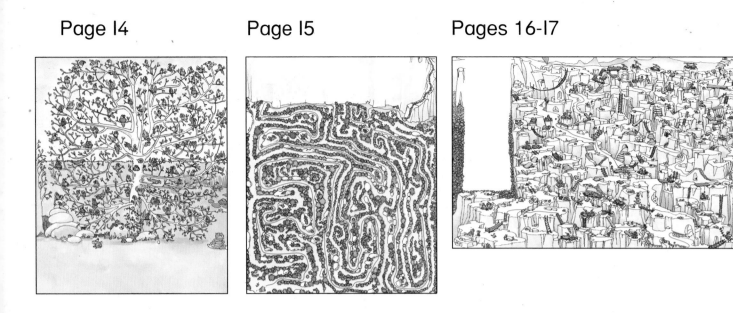

Pages 18-19

Page 20

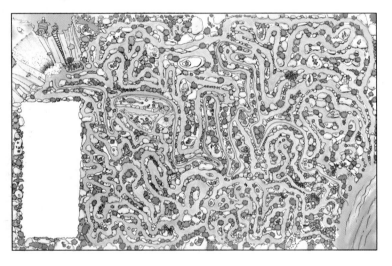

Page 21

Page 22

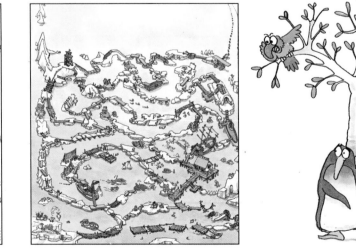